Bears in Pairs

By Niki Yektai • Pictures by Diane deGroat

Aladdin Books
Macmillan Publishing Company
New York

Collier Macmillan Canada
Toronto

Maxwell Macmillan
International Publishing Group
New York Oxford Singapore Sydney

For my father, Nicholas E. Kulukundis

N.Y.

Black bear

Brown bear

Up bear

Down bear

White bear

Green bear

King bear

Queen bear

Fat bear

Thin bear

Pink bear

Twin bear

Purple bear

Blue bear

Old bear

New bear

Orange bear

Small bear

Yellow bear

Tall bear

Red bear

Glad bear

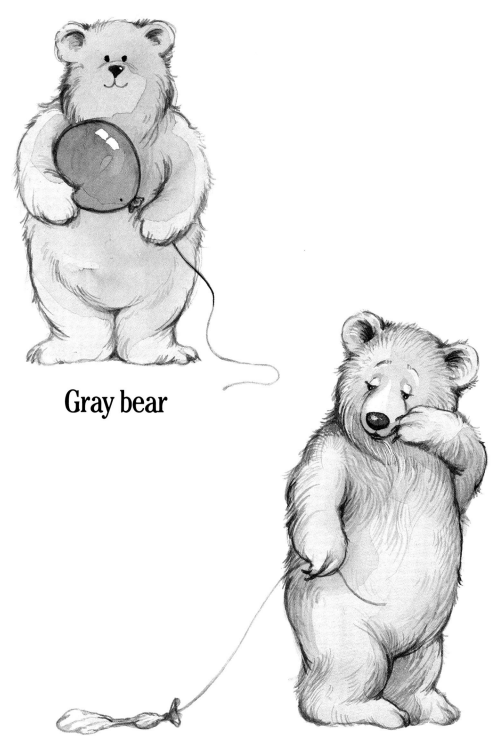

Gray bear

Sad bear

Fast bear

Slow bear

High bear

Low bear

Hairy bear

Scary bear

Silly bear

Frilly bear

Bear with rose

Bear with bows

Bear with flag

Bear with bag

Bear with spots

Bear with dots

Bear with tie

Bear with pie

Bear on bike

Bear in train

Bear in car

Bear in plane

Bear with hearts

Bear with tarts

Bear with sweets

Bear with treats

Hurry bears!

Hurry to…

Mary's tea party.

First Aladdin Books edition 1991   Text copyright © 1987 by Niki Yektai   Illustrations copyright © 1987 by Diane deGroat   All rights reserved. No part of this book may be reproduced or transmitted in any form or by any means, electronic or mechanical, including photocopying, recording, or by any information storage and retrieval system, without permission in writing from the Publisher.   Aladdin Books, Macmillan Publishing Company, 866 Third Avenue, New York, NY 10022   Collier Macmillan Canada, Inc., 1200 Eglinton Avenue East, Suite 200, Don Mills, Ontario M3C 3N1   Printed in the United States of America   A hardcover edition of *Bears in Paris* is available from Bradbury Press, an affiliate of Macmillan, Inc.   2   3   4   5   6   7   8   9   10

Library of Congress Cataloging-in-Publication Data   Yektai, Niki. Bears in pairs / by Niki Yektai; pictures by Diane deGroat.—1st Aladdin Books ed. p.   cm. Summary: Shows a multitude of bears, fat and thin, hairy and scary, with hearts and tarts, on their way to Mary's tea party. ISBN 0-689-71500-5 [1. Bears—Fiction. 2. Parties—Fiction. 3. Stories in rhyme.] I. De Groat, Denise, ill. II. Title. [PZ8.3.Y43Be   1991] [E]—dc20   91-229   CIP   AC